The Music Inside Me

Written and illustrated by fourth and fifth grade students
of Marvin Elementary School in Norwalk, Connecticut

Scholastic Inc.

New York Toronto London Auckland Sydney Mexico City New Delhi Hong Kong

Kids Are Authors ®
Books written by children for children

The Kids Are Authors ® Competition was established in 1986
to encourage children to read and to become involved in the creative process of writing.
Since then, thousands of children have written and illustrated books
as participants in the Kids Are Authors ® Competition.
The winning books in the annual competition are published by Scholastic Inc.
and are distributed by Scholastic Book Fairs throughout the United States.

For more information:
Kids Are Authors®
1080 Greenwood Blvd.
Lake Mary, FL 32746

Or visit our web site at:
www.scholastic.com/kidsareauthors

12 11 10 9 8 7 6 5 4 3 2 1

Cover and Book Design by Bill Henderson
Printed and bound in the U.S.A.

First Printing, June 2005

To our parents who taught us to listen
to the music inside our hearts

Left to right: Alex Libre, Kate Nelson, Gavin Nelson

Gavin and Kate Nelson are the authors and illustrators
of three books. *Ralph's Weird Week* and *Ralph Hates
Math* both won Honorable Mention Awards in the
Scholastic Kids Are Authors Competition in 2004
and 2005 respectively. *The Music Inside Me* is their
first book to win the Grand Prize in this prestigious
competition. Alex Libre joined Kate and Gavin to help
illustrate *The Music Inside Me.* Much of their
inspiration came from afternoons playing at the seashore.
Kate, Gavin, and Alex are students at
Marvin Elementary School and live in
Norwalk, Connecticut.

When I was a young girl, I lived by the water on a street called Seaside Place. At the end of my block stood an old, weather-beaten Victorian house that was said to be haunted. In it lived a crotchety, old man whose wife had died long ago. He was tall and skinny, with piercing blue eyes, and a long, white, scraggly beard that hung over his worn-out clothes. Back then, to us, he looked like he was at least 105 years old.

Everyday he'd sit on his porch with his right hand rummaging through a bucket while the fingers of his left hand made these strange, quick movements. While playing at the shore, my friends and I would look back at him on his porch, thinking he was the oldest, creepiest man we had ever seen.

One afternoon, during our daily game of "dare," it was decided that the loser would have to go talk to the old man. As always, being the youngest, I lost. That day changed my memories of Seaside Place forever. I am now 40 years old, and I still smile when I think of that afternoon and my first introduction to Charlie Blaine.

As I walked toward his porch, I trembled inside. The old man's eyes were closed, and he was humming while the fingers of his left hand were moving furiously. He was completely unaware of me. I tried coughing loudly to gain his attention, but he was lost in his own sounds.

I was so close that I could touch him. I could fee the butterflies in my stomach. I could feel my friends staring at me as they looked on in shock from the shore.

Taking a huge, deep breath, I tapped him on the shoulder. Startled, he jumped up, and I screamed. With one swift movement, he grabbed my arm so I couldn't run.

"Let go!" I shouted, as the tears began to well up in my eyes.

"Wait," he whispered with a voice as smooth as the sea. As I blinked back my tears, I could see the twinkle in his eyes and the smile on his wrinkled face. "You must be the loser of the game," he chuckled. "Did they dare you to come see the creepiest man?"

I could feel my face get red and hot. "How did you know that's what we call you?" I demanded.

"I might be old and creepy, but I haven't lost my hearing yet," he said still laughing. "Every day the wind blows out of the southwest, and the conversations of all you little rascals drift right onto my porch. But don't worry; your secrets are safe with me. In fact, I enjoy hearing your voices and laughter. It adds to the music inside me. And I'd enjoy it even more if you sat down with me and told me your name."

I could hear murmurings from the shore and then the scattering of feet as my friends ran home in disbelief. With my heart thumping, I told him my name was Jenny, and that I was seven years old and lived up the block. He introduced himself as Mr. Blaine, Charles Blaine, but said with a wink that his friends called him Charlie. Being a bold seven-year-old, I replied, "OK, Charlie, can I ask you a question? What are you doing with your fingers? Why do you move them around like that?"

"You are a bold young lady! But sit down, and I'll give you an answer." I tentatively sat on the porch railing as Charlie began his story.

"Years ago, I was a world renowned cellist. I played for hundreds of audiences in 23 different countries. As I grew old, I developed something called arthritis. My fingers became very stiff, and I was unable to continue performing. But the music is still inside me, and when I hum, my left hand can't help itself; it plays the notes. I think you kids talk about playing the air guitar. Well, I play the air cello!"

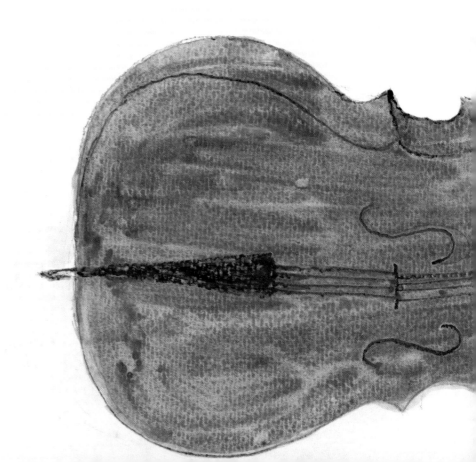

I had to get home for dinner but squeezed in one more question. I was curious about the old, faded bucket next to Charlie's creaking rocking chair. "What's in the bucket?" I asked.

"Ah, you are interested in my sea glass collection. You and your friends are not the only ones who walk along the beach. Before you were even born, I would take long walks along the rocky shore hunting for treasures discarded by the sea. Tomorrow, why don't you and your friends come visit this creepy, old man, and I'll tell you about my sea glass? That is, if your friends aren't too chicken," he added with a smile. So I went home eagerly awaiting the next day.

The following afternoon, my friends were still astonished by my bravery. As the daredevil of our group, I could now embarrass them into visiting Charlie. They trudged along behind me as we neared Charlie's house. "So, the motley crew is here," he said from his porch. "Come sit with a lonely old man. I'll enjoy the company, and you may learn something!"

I introduced Bobby, Alex, Kevin, and Susan, who were barely able to stammer, "Hello." With my dumbstruck friends being of no help, I blurted, "Can you show us your sea glass?"

"You'd like to see my treasures from the sea," Charlie responded. He bent over, picked up the bucket and set it on his lap with a groan. Holding a piece up to the light, he began, "You see, this piece, like every piece, is worn and tumbled, has traveled many miles, and has been bumped and banged over rocks and sand until beautifully polished. I like to think of it as being just like me," he chortled. "Every time I pick up a piece, it reminds me of the sights, sounds, and memories of my life at the seashore."

19

I reached into the bucket and pulled out a beautiful red piece and asked what it reminded him of. "Oh," he said, "if I close my eyes, I see the red, sunburned cheeks of my daughter as she skipped gracefully along the sea wall many years ago."

"How old is your daughter now?" Bobby asked.

"She is 47 years old, and she has a family of her own," Charlie said softly. "Unfortunately for me, they live far away in Utah. But I love hearing the chatter of my grandchildren on the phone. It's part of the music inside me."

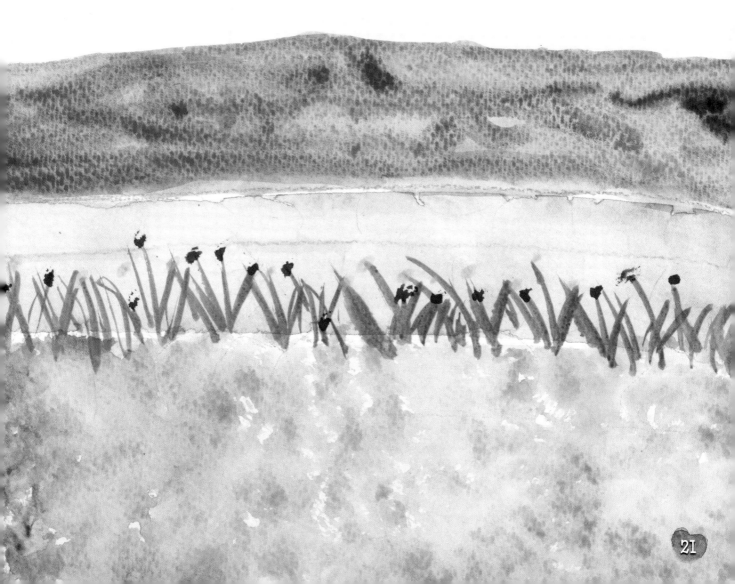

"What about this piece?" Alex chimed in.

"That lovely sea green color reminds me of the beautiful sparkle in my wife's green eyes."

Everybody started digging into the bucket and asking questions all at once. It soon became a wild chorus of voices asking, "What about this one, and that one?"

Charlie quieted us all down with a holler. "One at a time!
Ah, Susan, that blue piece reminds me of a clear blue water of
the harbor. And Kevin, that purple piece reminds me of the
gorgeous winter sky at sunset."

I asked about an amber colored piece. "That is the color of my cello, which created the most wonderful music for me for many years. When I see that piece, I think of my first performance at Carnegie Hall."

"Don't you get sad when you think of these memories?" I asked.

"Yes, this is sadness, Jenny, but these memories are inside me; my daughter, my wife, my music—they are inside me. They are always a part of me, and will always be part of the music inside my heart."

Bobby had run down to the beach and excitedly came back
with a piece of sea glass for Charlie's collection. "This, Bobby,"
he said, "this one is young like you. It's edges are still rough.
It needs to travel more places, be bumped around, be
smoothed and polished. Then it can go in my bucket."
Charlie picked up a handful of sea glass and said softly,
"You know what I like best—listen." As he dropped the sea
glass back into the bucket, it made the most wonderful plinking
noise. "It's the music of sea glass."

From that day on, we spent afternoons with Charlie listening to fascinating stories of his life. What he liked best of all was hearing us coming up the dirt road chattering away and laughing. He always said it added to the music in his heart.

One day we arrived and there was a "For Sale" sign in front of his house. With downcast eyes, Charlie explained that because he was getting older, his daughter thought it would be best if he lived with her. He was glad to be moving closer to his daughter but very sad to be leaving Seaside Place. We were disappointed too. He was no longer a creepy old man, but had become a dear friend.

FOR SALE

Before he moved, we all worked together on a gift for Charlie. The day he was leaving, we sat together on his porch. He told us to never lose the music inside our hearts. A gentle breeze blew just as he opened his gift, a wind chime made of sea glass. The chime's soft plinking music brought tears to his eyes, and he said one last time, "This will be a part of the music in my heart." We hugged goodbye, and that was the last time I saw Charlie Blaine.

Years later, a package arrived for me. It was from Utah, from Charlie's daughter. I opened it to see the long-forgotten, sea glass wind chime with a note that read:

Mr. Blaine passed away last month. Before he died, he asked me to send the wind chime to the young girl who added much music to his life.

It now hangs on my porch.